NOT MY IDEA

A BOOK ABOUT WHITENESS

Written and illustrated by
Anastasia Higginbotham

dottir
press

Published in 2018 by Dottir Press
33 Fifth Avenue
New York, NY 10003

Dottirpress.com

FIRST PAPERBACK EDITION
First printing: August 2020

Illustration and design by Anastasia Higginbotham
Photography by Alexa Hoyer
Production by Drew Stevens

Special thanks to Jennifer Baumgardner, Drew Stevens, Abraham Higginbotham,
Lisa Daniels, and Jon Luongo.
Pencil drawing on page 11 by Sabatino Luongo Higginbotham.
Additional editing by Lionel Luongo Higginbotham.

Library of Congress Cataloging-in-Publication Data is available for this title.
ISBN 978-1-9483-4040-3

Printed in the United States of America by Worzalla

In a 1993 interview, Toni Morrison said about racism in America: "White people have a very, very serious problem, and **they** should start thinking about what **they** can do about it." She added, "Take **me** out of it." Those words landed in me as a direct command.

I made this book for my own white sons with help from their teachers and mine. It's dedicated to the Brooklyn Free School, where my family was first called upon to engage with whiteness in order to dismantle white supremacy.

Deepest thanks to:

Ben Howort

Rev. angel Kyodo williams

Loretta Ross

Anyanwu Uwa

Randy Clancy

Noleca Anderson Radway

...it's usually
because they're
scared too.

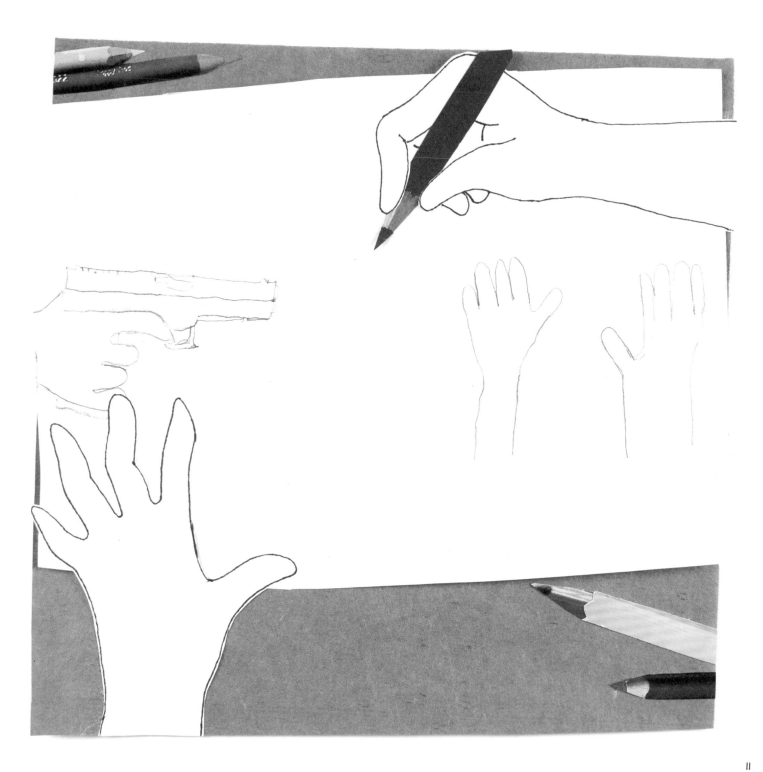

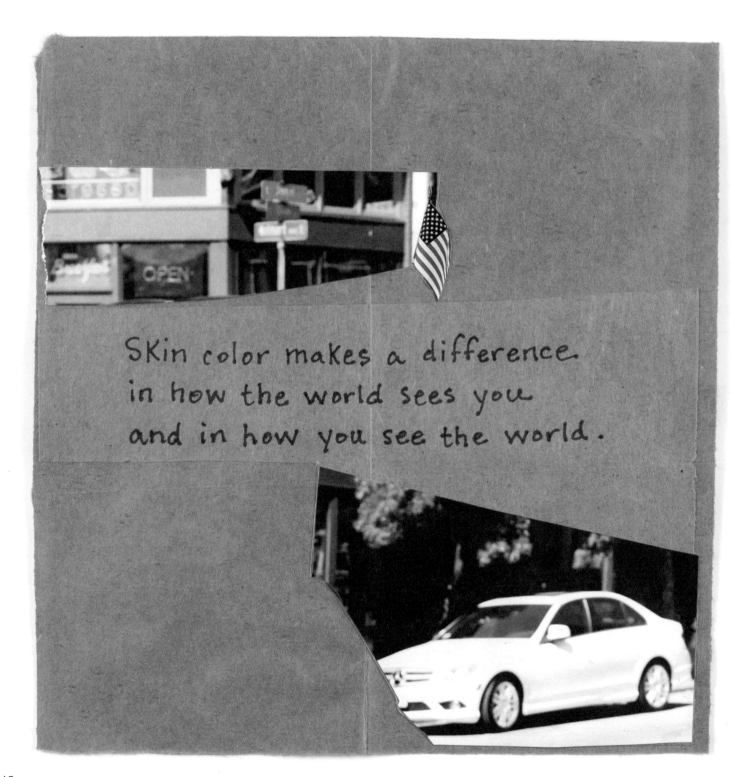

Skin color makes a difference
in how the world sees you
and in how you see the world.

13

It makes a difference in how

much
trouble
seems
to
find you
or
let
you
be.

$8

$10

In stores,
  in cars,
on sidewalks,
  at school —

  your skin color
  affects the most
  ordinary daily
  experiences,

      including...

... which neighborhoods welcome you.

19

You may get the message
that racism is happening only
to Black and brown people.

—mostly by
refusing
to look
at it .

Come away
from the
TV, now.

LooK—
I made your
favorite.

You can
face
this.

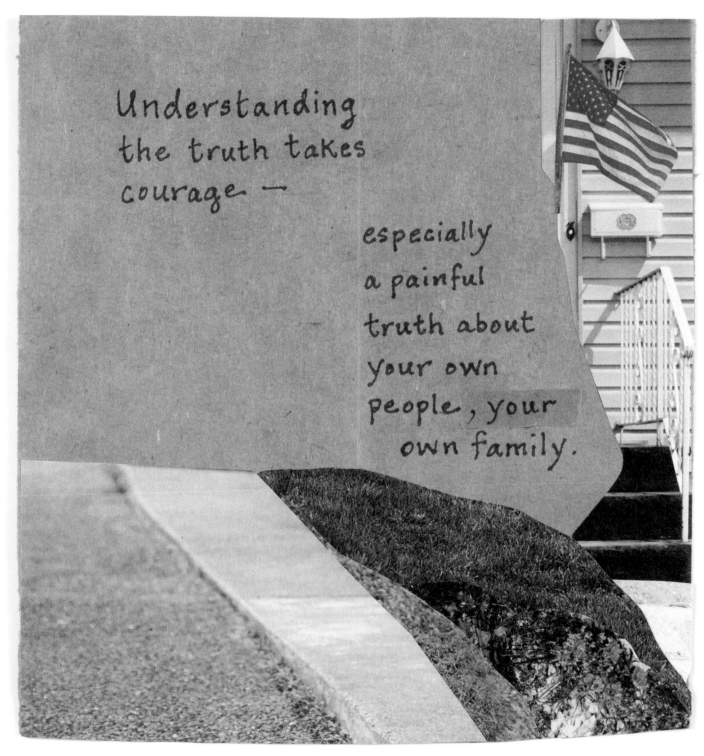

Understanding
the truth takes
courage —

especially
a painful
truth about
your own
people, your
own family.

Even people
you love
may behave
in ways
that show...

...they think *they* are the good ones.

Racism was not your idea. You don't need to defend it.

I'll be over here if you need me, okay?

You can bring your curiosity to learn about it and see that it's true.

In the United States of America, white people have committed outrageous crimes against Black people for four hundred years.

All along, every step of the way, people who love justice and love each other have been fighting back.

Many white people did things they **never** should have done.

Bank Loan $$$

DENIED

denied opportunity

NOTICE OF EVICTION

denied housing

Voter Registration TEST Parts A,B,C Pages I-4 Sections I-20

215 J

denied voting rights

Many other white people failed to see the problem with this.

exploited the love and labor of Black women

Yes, ma'am.

These choices put wealth and power into white hands, homes, and neighborhoods.

Some white people joined the leaders of Black liberation.*

Angelina Grimké and Sarah Grimké, 1838

Abolitionists, Suffragists, Sisters

Julian Bond and members of the Student Nonviolent Coordinating Committee, 1963

*liberation = love + freedom

Nina Simone, 1967

Nuns and fellow marchers
on the
Selma to Montgomery
March, 1965

Colin Kaepernick
kneels, 2017

John Lewis and
fellow demonstrators kneel, 1962

37

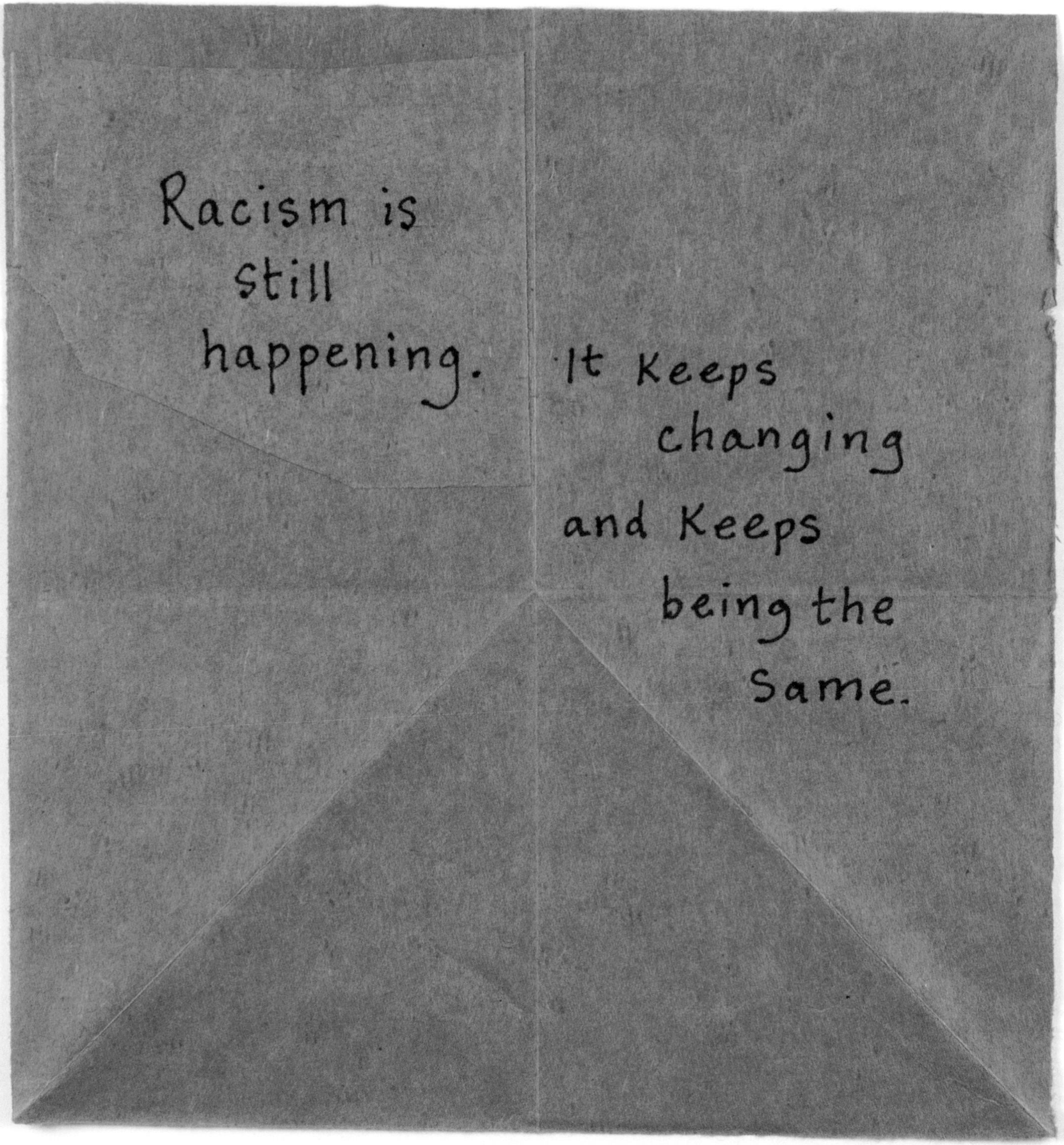

Racism is
still
happening.

It Keeps
changing
and Keeps
being the
Same.

And yet...
just being here,
alive in this moment,
you have a chance
to care about this,
to connect.

41

...like breaking.

Go with your instincts on this one.
Racial justice is possible.

your history's not all written yet.

What do you
want it to say?

the end.

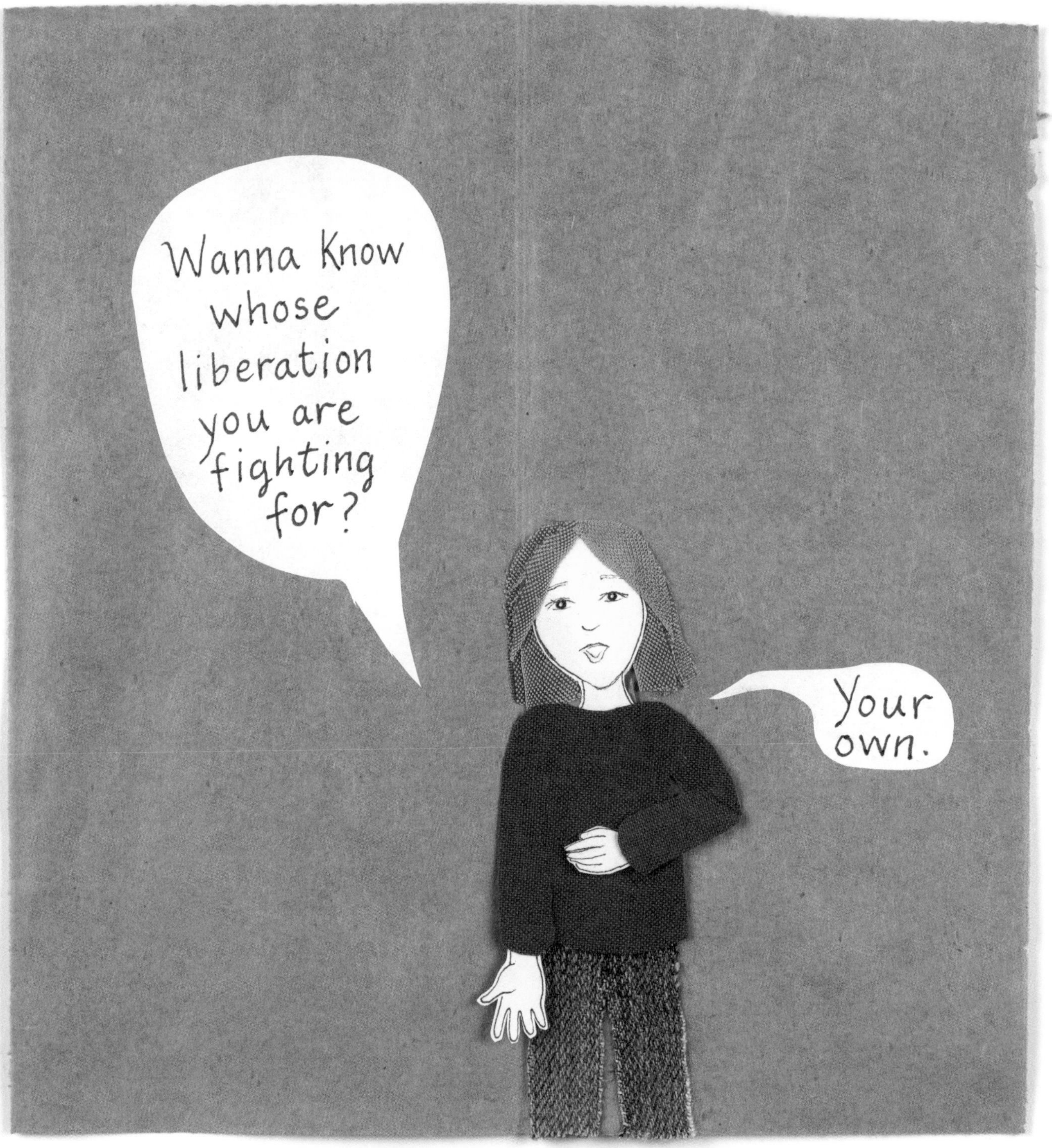
Wanna Know whose liberation you are fighting for?
Your own.

White supremacy has been lying to kids for centuries.

White supremacy is pretend. But the consequences are real.

dangerous

The truth is much simpler.

not dangerous

WHITENESS IS
A BAD DEAL.

It always was.

Dude, we can
see your
pointy tail.

You
can be
WHITE

without
signing
on to
whiteness.

Juliette Hampton Morgan

Do not mess with me.

Born 1914

Died 1957

...was a white librarian who fought for racial justice in Montgomery, Alabama.

When Juliette was riding the bus and the white driver would refuse to pick up a Black bus rider - even after he collected their fare ($$$) - Juliette would pull the emergency cord and raise H-E-double-hockey-sticks until the driver did his job.

This was an act of love, for herself and for the community to which she belonged.

What she did is called: disrupting white supremacy.

GROW justice
inside yourself like a bean sprout in a milk carton
What if it dies?
plant it again
NEVER
STOP
PLANTING
JUSTICE

A strong, internal sense of justice will not fail you—

even when a lack of justice in the world does.

Innocence
is
overrated.

Knowledge is Power

Color this in ↗

Get some. Grow wise.
Make history.

Some people who *should be alive in this moment* are not. And *that* hurts.

Write their names here. Draw them a picture.

Show what's in you, even if you feel sad, or angry, or VERY SAD & VERY ANGRY (this paper absorbs tears).

And if it's joy that you feel, let it flow.

Dismantling white supremacy is a choice
(followed by another and another . . .).

It is a way of being.
Every day we get to plant justice instead.

Here are some ideas to help you connect with your own choices
and the justice you want to grow in the world.

Wanna end racism immediately?

So do I but...

Hold up.

That is not how this works.
It is what it is -- for now.

Can't we get a new one of these?

100% USA

Nope. That's our only one.

Dang! But this one's all full of racism.

PREPARE TO BE SURPRISED by who will and who won't discuss racism with you.

That's not polite to talk about.

That's none of your business.

[silence]

BEYOND THIS POINT UNSAFE

Seek truth and sanctuary in books and libraries.

LIKE A LOT OF SECRET WEAPONS:

Racism hides.

Here's a code to find it:

BELIEVE IT **2** see IT

In stores
On sidewalks
At school
Visiting relatives
Riding in cars

Get ready to FLIP

what happens when U R Black and a person of color in these places?

what happens when U R white in these places?

Just see — for now. See what you see.

WHAT if

every time someone mentions racism, a lot of feelings jump up in you?

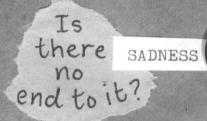

I know how *that* feels.

ANGER

I didn't do it!

I did do it.

SHAME

Is there no end to it?

SADNESS

There must be a reason for it.

CONFUSION

Gather up all these feelings and more.

Hey, c'mere everybody.

jumpy feelings

OKay, now STAY. You're ugly but you're mine ♡

Take care not to aim the feelings at those who did not cause them.

Black and Brown People

I'm afraid of making a mistake.

What do you usually do when you make a mistake?

Say, I'm sorry.

So do that.

Learn for next time.

Your history is not written yet. What do you want it to say?

Here is a place where you can write, draw, collage,
or envision an answer to this.

How do you want to make history with your individual choices
(the ones you make for you)?

How do you want to make history as part of a community and collective
(the ways we move together)?